FUCK ALL THE WAY OFF

Triggered Animals

A SCORNFUL SWEARING ADULT COLORING BOOK

All vintage images are from the British Library on-line collection
found at www.flickr.com/photos/britishlibrary

instagram

Post coloring pages on instagram @colormenaughtybooks
#triggeredanimals

MW00890557

OTHER BOOKS BY COLOR ME NAUGHTY

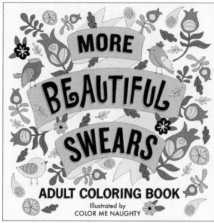

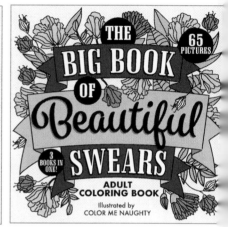

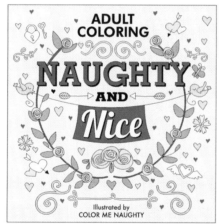

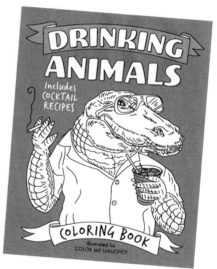

Copyright © 2018 by Color Me Naughty

ISBN 9781729498088

OH, YOU THINK I GIVE A SHIT? HOW CUTE.

COLORED BY

DATE

FUCK YOU, MONDAY

COLORED BY
_____

DATE
_____

FUCK YOU, MONDAY

COLORED BY

DATE

ADIOS
BITCHACHOS

COLORED BY

DATE

THIS IS A
REAL FUCKING
SHITSHOW

COLORED BY

DATE

COLORED BY

DATE

I DO A THING
CALLED
WHAT I WANT

COLORED BY

DATE

YOU CAN KISS MY SWEET ASS

COLORED BY

_____

DATE

ONCE UPON A TIME, FUCK YOU. THE END

COLORED BY

DATE

THIS IS AN UNBELIEVABLE AMOUNT OF BULLSHIT

COLORED BY

DATE

COLORED BY

DATE

NOT TODAY
SATAN

COLORED BY

DATE

READ A
FUCKING
BOOK

COLORED BY

DATE

KARMA'S A
BITCH

COLORED BY

DATE

HONESTLY, I HAVE NO FUCKS LEFT TO GIVE.

COLORED BY

_____

DATE

COLORED BY

DATE

FUCK OFF.
I MEAN,
GOOD MORNING.

COLORED BY

DATE

BITCH, PLEASE

COLORED BY

DATE

COLORED BY

DATE

GET
FUUUUUCKED

COLORED BY

DATE

JUDGE ME

WHEN YOU ARE FUCKING PERFECT.

COLORED BY

DATE

I'D AGREE WITH YOU BUT THEN WE'D BOTH BE WRONG.

COLORED BY

_____

DATE

_____

COLORED BY

DATE

RESTING
BITCH FACE

COLORED BY

DATE

COLORED BY

DATE

YOU NEED
A HIGH FIVE
IN THE
FUCKING FACE.

COLORED BY

DATE

GET YOUR SHIT TOGETHER

COLORED BY

DATE

COLORED BY

DATE

FUCK ALL THE
WAY OFF

COLORED BY

_____

DATE

ENOUGH OF YOUR DOUCHEBAGGERY

COLORED BY

DATE

SO TRIGGERED
RIGHT NOW

COLORED BY

DATE

HOW ABOUT
FUCKING
YOURSELF?

COLORED BY

DATE

GET BENT

COLORED BY

DATE

MAYBE
SWEARING
WILL HELP

COLORED BY

DATE

I HOPE
ONE DAY
YOU
CHOKE
ON ALL
THAT
SHIT
YOU
TALK

COLORED BY

DATE

YOU'RE
CANCELLED

COLORED BY

DATE

REMEMBER WHEN I ASKED FOR YOUR OPINION? YEAH, ME NEITHER.

COLORED BY

DATE

MESS WITH MY KIDS &
I WILL FUCK YOU UP

COLORED BY

DATE

I HONESTLY DON'T GIVE 2 SHITS ABOUT MY HAIR TODAY

COLORED BY

DATE

GET WRECKED

COLORED BY

DATE

Manufactured by Amazon.ca
Bolton, ON

10360956R00049